How to Outsmart a

ninja

Eric Braun

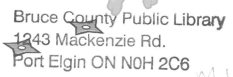

**BLACK
RABBIT
BOOKS**

Hi Jinx is published by Black Rabbit Books
P.O. Box 3263, Mankato, Minnesota, 56002.
www.blackrabbitbooks.com
Copyright © 2020 Black Rabbit Books

Jen Besel, editor; Michael Sellner, designer;
Omay Ayres, photo researcher

Library of Congress Cataloging-in-Publication Data
Names: Braun, Eric, 1971- author.
Title: How to outsmart a ninja / by Eric Braun.
Description: Mankato, Minnesota : Black Rabbit Books,
[2020] | Series: Hi Jinx. How to outsmart ... | Includes
bibliographical references and index.
Identifiers: LCCN 2018015182 (print) | LCCN 2018024051
(ebook) | ISBN 9781680729290 (e-book) |
ISBN 9781680729238 (library binding) | ISBN
9781644660614 (paperback)
Subjects: LCSH: Ninja—Juvenile humor. |
Wit and humor, Juvenile.
Classification: LCC PN6231.N65 (ebook) |
LCC PN6231.N65 B73 2020 (print) |
DDC 818/.602—dc23
LC record available at
https://lccn.loc.gov/2018015182

Printed in China. 1/19

Image Credits

iStock: Adelevin, 16 (kids);
Dezein, 15 (phone);
erhui1979, 6–7 (keyhole);
Shutterstock: Aluna1,
12–13 (bkgd), 19 (steps);
artpustovit, 7 (kids); Blue
Planet Earth, 13 (girl);
BlueRingMedia, 15 (boy);
Christos Georghiou, 4 (torn paper); ekler, 10 (torn paper);
Freestyle_stock_photo, Cover (bkgd); 15 (phone bkgd); Funny Drew,
3, 16, 21 (bkgd); Giingerann, 11 (ninja); GraphicsRF, 12 (tacks); Ken
Benner, 5 (chair); LintangDesign, 2–3 (ninja); mark stay, 18–19 (door);
Memo Angeles, Cover (ninja), 4 (ninja) 15 (ninja), 16 (ninja), 19 (boys);
NoPainNoGain, Cover (chemistry bkgd); opicobello, 10 (torn paper), 12
(marker stroke); Pasko Maksim, Back Cover, 23, 24 (torn paper); pitju, 4,
13, 17, 21 (curled paper); Ron Dale, 5, 9, 13, 14, 20 (marker stroke); Ron
Leishman, 8 (all); Sarawut Padungkwan, 1 (bl & br), 18–19 (ninja), 23 (ninja);
sundatoon, 1 (boy); TAW4, 12 (ninja); Tomacco, 21 (ninja); Tonov, 6 (ninja);
VectorShots, 5 (girl); Verzzh, 5 (book) Every effort has been made to contact
copyright holders for material reproduced in this book. Any omissions will be
rectified in subsequent printings if notice is given to the publisher.

Contents

Chapter 1

Deadly Sneaker

Imagine this. You're sitting alone in your living room. You're reading a book (because you're smart). The house is totally quiet. Suddenly, a person dressed in black pajamas leaps out. You let out a bloodcurdling scream.

Hold on. Relax. This scene isn't happening right now. But it could happen someday. You could come face-to-face with a ninja at any time.

Prepare Yourself

When a ninja sneaks up, *nobody* hears it. That is, until it's too late. A ninja's job is to learn people's secrets. Do you have any secrets? You know, like where your mom hides the cookies. Or who your best friend has a crush on.

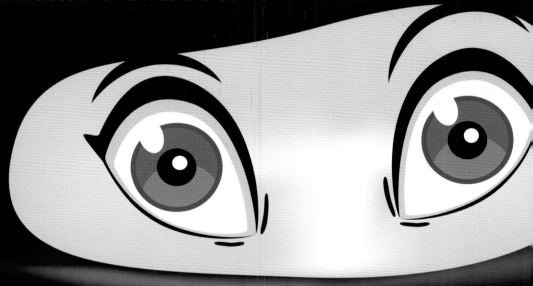

If you have **classified** info like that, watch out. Ninja might come after you. And that's why you need to know how to outsmart them.

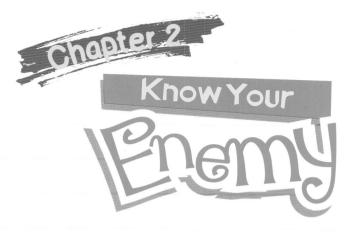

Chapter 2

Know Your

Enemy

It's important to learn all you can about ninja. You'll have a better chance to get away. The problem is that it's hard to learn about ninja. Nobody knows who they are. The person sitting next to you could be a ninja. Watch for clues. Do they have soft footsteps? Do they disappear at **random** times? Hmmmmmmm …

Ninja in history are known for their fighting. They trained in **martial arts**. Are you a black belt in anything? If not, you really need this book.

Working in the Dark

We do know ninja are good at doing things in the dark. Most people can't see well at night. But ninja train hard to improve their **vision**. In fact, they train all their senses, even smell.

You need to know ninja often wear **disguises**. Sometimes they wear black pajamas. But don't be fooled. Ninja don't want bedtime stories.

Their black pajamas are traditionally called shinobi shozoku. The clothes aren't really pajamas. They are loose and good for doing fighting moves.

Be sure you're dealing with a ninja
and not your dad going to bed.

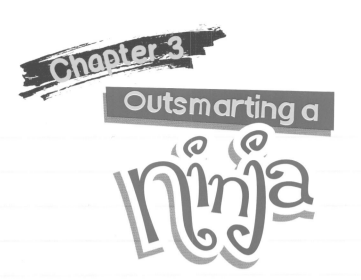

Chapter 3

Outsmarting a ninja

So you have a ninja problem. Here are some ideas to outsmart him or her. First, don't try hiding in the dark. Ninja can see you. And don't try sneaking away. Ninja are expert sneakers.

Try dumping thumbtacks all over the floor. (Make sure the pointy ends are up!) The tacks will poke right through the ninja's soft slippers.

Use the Flash!

Another idea is to use your phone or camera. Have the flash on, and wait. When you think the ninja is in the room, snap a bunch of shots. The flash will blind the ninja. And you'll have a photo of him or her. Put the pic on social media. You can't be a ninja if everyone knows who you are.

Tip

Don't ask for a selfie with the ninja. That's probably dangerous.

Pajama Party!

Here's a fun way to **distract** a ninja. Have a pajama party! Invite friends over, and pop some popcorn. Put on a scary movie. The ninja is already in pajamas. He or she won't be able to **resist** hanging out with you.

Do not play a ninja movie.

Catch the Ninja

Use a ninja's excellent hearing against him or her. First, record yourself talking. Make it natural. (Better yet, record a conversation with your bestie.) Put the recording in a room with a door. Then play back the recording while you hide in another room. The ninja will follow the sounds of the voices. When he or she enters the room, slam and lock the door!

Ninja are sneaky. But so are you. With these tips, you can outsmart any ninja who tries to sneak up on you.

Chapter 4

Get in on the Lo-Hi-Jinx

Of course, ninja aren't sneaking around your house at night. But ninja in history did go on spy missions. They trained their bodies, including their senses.

Like a ninja, you can learn to see better in the dark. This skill could be useful for getting midnight snacks. Practice by sitting in a totally dark room. Pick out shapes, outlines, and movement. For faster results, wear an eye patch like a pirate. Take it off when you go into the dark. That eye is already used to the dark.

Don't use your new skills for evil.

Take It One Step More

1. Because they are so secretive, nobody knows if ninja exist today. Do some research on your own. Do you think there are ninja now?

2. What are some other jobs that require someone to be quick, quiet, and sneaky?

3. People love ninja books, movies, and costumes. Why do you think that is?

GLOSSARY

classified (KLAS-uh-fahyd)—kept secret from all but a few people

disguise (dis-GYZ)—a change to the usual appearance of someone or something so that people won't recognize it

distract (deh-STRAKT)—to draw attention to something else

martial art (MAR-shul ART)—any of several arts of combat and self-defense (such as karate or tae kwon do) that are widely practiced as a sport

random (RAN-duhm)—chosen, done, or ordered without a particular plan or pattern

resist (ree-ZIST)—to fight against something or try to stop it

vision (VIH-zhun)—the act or power of seeing

BOOKS

Matthews, Rupert. *Ninjas.* History's Fearless Fighters. New York: Gareth Stevens Publishing, 2016.

Roza, Greg. *Ninjas.* Warriors around the World. New York: Britannica Educational Publishing in association with Rosen Educational Services, 2017.

Terp, Gail. *Ninja.* History's Warriors. Mankato, MN: Black Rabbit Books, 2020.

WEBSITES

Ninja Encyclopedia
www.ninjaencyclopedia.com

What Is a Ninja?
iganinja.jp/en/about/ninja.html

What's Ninja?
ninja-official.com/whats-ninja?lang=en

INDEX